The Space Between

Choices Collection

A short Story Collection

By Tina Linn

I'd like to give my thanks to all who made these short stories possible. Because without the support in my life, this wouldn't be possible. Thank You!

Table of Contents

The First Hike

Short Story 1

The First Hike

That should do it.

Finally caught up on the reports, Vincent Groober leaned back in his chair, relieved to be done. Like everyone in his field, he despised the paperwork aspect of his job. Fortunately, he spent most of his time on call for Search and Rescue or guiding people around Acadia National Park. It was far more rewarding than doing these dreaded things.

I wonder if our newest recruit will feel the same way? Though he knew a little about Rodney Johnson from the numerous times he had come to them for guidance around the park, he didn't really know him personally. The kid was easy-going and polite with the guides, but Vincent had noticed that if anyone belittled a guide in front of him, the boy's calm demeanor would sharpen subtly. He didn't lose his temper, but a quiet intensity would emerge, enough to make someone think twice about underestimating him.

He was pondering how the boy could be so wise when a knock at the door pulled him out of his thoughts. "It's open."

Rodney nervously poked his head in. "Y-you wanted to see me, Mr. Groober?"

"I did," Vincent said with a warm smile. "Come in. Have a seat."

Hesitantly, Rodney obliged. No surprise since most of the time when a boss called someone into their office, it was no different than a student being sent to the principal's office. Something that's probably still fresh since he graduated a couple of months before his eighteenth birthday last month. And with some situations where they'll need to talk in private, he needed to get him comfortable as soon as possible.

"First of all," Vincent began, "I wanted to welcome you to the team. We're all excited to have you here."

"Thanks." He was happy to see some of the nervous energy melt away from his posture. "I'm excited to be here too."

"Second of all, I know you've hiked and explored much of Acadia as a visitor, but you still need to partner up with someone to learn the ropes of guiding. Once your partner feels you're ready, we'll see how you do taking charge of large groups and leading solo ones. Sound good?"

"Sounds good. So when do I get to meet my partner?"

Vincent's grin widened as he got to his feet. "You're looking at him."

Rodney's jaw nearly hit the floor. "O-Oh... uh, okay."

"Don't worry," Vincent chuckled, patting Rodney's shoulder as he skirted his desk. "I'm no tyrant teacher. At least, I haven't been called that- as far as I know."

"T-That's not it! I'm just... surprised, is all."

"Surprised because I'm the boss?" Rodney sheepishly shrugged as they left the room. "Well, believe it or not, this boss loves being out there with the rest of the team. Plus, it's better for you to have me as your partner than the only other option. Though he's a close second to me, he's not really suited to train new recruits—not unless I don't care whether or not they quit before they even start."

"Is he really that bad?"

"Well," Vincent carefully responded, "it depends on perspective. He's top-notch at guiding and getting the job done— but grumpy with new guides. That's why I sent him with the earlier group."

"You mean Casey?" Rodney's eyes widened in surprise when he confirmed it. "But he's usually so nice. And helpful too."

"Wait until you're around him as his greenhorn equal. But don't worry, he's only that way for the first year. Right, Rose?"

Rose Brandy, a ten-year guide veteran, chuckled as they stopped next to her desk. "You're right, usually. But not this time, Boss."

Vincent blinked. "What do you mean, not this time!?"

"When Rodney came in ready for work, Casey was the first to congratulate him—and offer help if he needed it."

"Wow. That's a first." He turned toward Rodney. "You must've made a good impression when you hiked and climbed with him."

Rodney gave a small smile. "I took his expert advice to heart whenever he was my guide, is all. He's also the one who suggested I should put in an application. However, he instructed me to omit his name from the referral. Said he'd rather not have everyone thinking he's gotten soft."

"Casey? Soft?" Vincent burst out laughing. "Only if you think hedgehogs' quills are soft."

Casey Randle had always been—and probably always would be—the most stubborn employee he'd ever had. Having been part of the team for sixteen years, nearly as long as Vincent himself, Casey wasn't one for being anything but cantankerous with new recruits. Though, like Rodney had pointed out, he was an excellent guide.

Well, whatever lessons Rodney had taken to heart, Vincent was glad his oldest employee had pre-approved him. It made his job easier on so many levels. He wouldn't have to worry when it came to assigning the two together later on.

Rodney relaxed. "So what path are we taking?"

"The Norumbega Mountain Loop," Vincent explained. "Our customer has a young child and has done *some* hiking with her."

"Sounds good. Should I bring extra snacks and water, just in case?"

"It doesn't hurt to be a little overprepared. But best to bring a fishing rod too."

"Already packed."

"Really?" Vincent raised an eyebrow.

Rodney gave a confirming nod. "Thanks to Casey, I know it's essential. Along with a reusable water bottle with a filter, a first-aid kit, and some simple wraps."

"Emergency blanket, knife, and rope?"

"Packed. You can never be too careful—even on a simple path. You never know if or when things are gonna go south, though the odds are low."

Vincent's smile grew. "Now I see how you already won Casey over." As guides, it was their job to be prepared for all sorts of scenarios while carrying as little as possible. Though the likelihood of needing most of it was slim, it was always better to have it and not need it than to suffer when something went awry. He was glad Rodney had already learned that lesson the smart way.

***

This must be them. Anxiously awaiting getting his first on-the-job training, Rodney watched a white Ford Escape pull up. He knew from the trouble he'd caused his dad as a child that not every kid handled hikes or camping trips easily. He'd whine and run off whenever he could—until he learned his lesson the hard way.

Some kids were easier, though, like his younger brother, Wade, who was a dream to be around in the wilderness. Always eager to explore, never whining, always ready to learn. He hoped this little one would be like Wade, rather than his former self.

The driver's side opened, and a brunette-haired woman stepped out, dressed appropriately for Maine's weather: a lightweight hiking shirt, convertible pants, and sturdy boots. To his relief, the little girl hopping out the back door wore a pink-and-white version of her mother's outfit—and a cute little backpack. When his boss mentioned the mom had stressed her child's hiking experience, Rodney had worried it might mean city parks only. He was glad he was wrong.

The hiking experience was even more confirmed with the backpack the mom put on. It wasn't overstuffed like most he'd seen. It seemed half full like his and his boss'. He wouldn't be surprised that she had a fishing rod too.

"Miss Briers, I presume?" Vincent held out a hand with a smile. "I'm Vincent Groober."

"Please, call me Yolanda," Yolanda said, clasping his hand. "Pleased to meet you in person, Vincent."

"Likewise." He turned his attention to Rodney. "Yolanda, meet our newest member."

"Ah, the one that started today, right?"

"That's me." He shook her hand. "I'm Rodney Johnson."

"Pleased to make your acquaintance, Rodney."

Rodney nodded and turned his attention to the little girl. His smile widened as he knelt down. "Well, hello there."

The little girl shyly half hid behind her Mom. "Hi."

"What's your name?"

"Jenny."

"Jenny? That's a pretty name. Well, Jenny. Are you ready to go hiking?"

Jenny gave a small nod, hiding fully behind her mom. Rodney chuckled at the adorability of it. He suddenly couldn't wait to see how much of a mountain goat she really was.

***

Ready, they hopped into their vehicles and headed to the start of Norumbega Mountain Loop. A short ride later, they spotted the other guide's and customers' vehicles. A bit surprising, considering they'd been gone for four hours on a simple two-and-a-half-hour round-trip hike.

But some people enjoyed lingering at the turnaround point. Lower Hadlock Pond was a beautiful location, after all. So Vincent wasn't too worried. And besides, Casey was one of the best guides on his team. If anything happened, he'd handle it with precision.

On the trail, he was pleased to see Jenny having a blast. Starting at the Goat Trail, he and Yolanda laughed as the little girl and Rodney played "mountain goat" up the steep ascent. Then, on the descent, they pretended to step into a magically enchanted forest filled with unicorns and fairies.

What made it all even better were the little details Rodney pointed out along the way. Some good examples were the red fox and the eastern milk snake, both well hidden among the trees and shrubbery. He even pointed out a dragonfly that even Vincent had nearly missed. The boy was observant, that was for sure.

Yolanda leaned close and whispered, "And who's teaching who?"

Vincent chuckled, "I'm starting to wonder. He's been hiking all over since he was young, so I'm not surprised he knows so much. But I didn't expect him to be a natural guide out of the gate."

"Or is this great with kids?"

"Or that." Vincent agreed. He had known Rodney had a little brother, but he hadn't seen how well they got along. If this was any indication, Rodney was a great older brother.

***

Smiling like a goof, Rodney watched as Jenny and Yolanda enjoyed the view of Lower Hadlock Pond. He had a blast playing with the little girl on the trail. Something he had hoped would happen, though he hadn't expected it.

"You're very good with kids."

"I'm used to them." Rodney shrugged as he glanced at his boss. "Wade has always enjoyed going on hikes and camping trips with Dad and me. Though it always gets interesting when he brings his rambunctious friends."

Vincent chuckled at the look on his face. "I'm guessing 'rambunctious' is an understatement?"

"Depends on whether or not you think their wanting to ride a wild moose or a bear fits that profile."

He gaped in horror. "You have to deal with that!?" He groaned at Rodney's confirmed nod. "You're a lot more relaxed about those types of brats than I would be. Golly, Rodney!"

"Eh," Rodney shrugged. "It's better than dealing with a whiny butt runaway. Gotta say, my parents are grateful I fell out of that phase."

And so am I.

"You!? Whiny in nature!?" Vincent shook his head. "I can't really say I believe that one."

"Oh, trust me. I was." Rodney chuckled. He was about to explain further when rustling from behind them made his chest tighten and the hairs on his neck spike. Something was wrong. Whirling around, he scanned every tree, every shadow, trying to pinpoint the source.

"Rodney?" Vincent's voice dropped to a whisper. "What is it?"

"I'm not sure..." Rodney carefully replied, his muscles tensing. "But... something doesn't feel right." Though he expected to see a bear or a moose causing the unease, he found neither. What he saw instead was just as chilling.

Sunlight glinted off a metallic object peeking from behind a tree. A gun barrel, aimed directly at Yolanda and Jenny. Time slowed as Rodney's stomach dropped. His hands shot forward, legs pumping before his mind even caught up.

"GUN-" he yelled.

Pain exploded across his side as the sharp crack echoed, but Rodney didn't falter. Instinct took over, limbs moving before thought. He lunged, ushering the two toward the nearest trees for cover. Every second stretched impossibly long, every heartbeat deafening.

Protect them. Don't think. Just move.

***

Why is this happening!?

Drawing his concealed weapon, Vincent fired in the direction of their attacker as he keyed his radio. "Rose! Rose! Pick up! Over." He dropped to a knee just as the attacker swung their weapon and fired again.

"I read you, Boss!" Rose's voice crackled through. "What's going on? Over."

"We're being shot at. Call law enforcement- now."

"Copy that. Calling it in." The attacker ducked and bolted. With another shot, not to hit, but to ensure whoever it was kept going. Then he sprinted toward the others.

Relief hit first. Rodney's instincts had been right: get those under their care out of sight, not chase the threat. It was exactly what Vincent would've ordered. He opened his mouth to say as much and froze. A dark red stain spread across Rodney's back, blooming through the fabric. He'd been shot.

"Rodney," Vincent gasped, dropping beside him.

"It's just a graze," Rodney forced out with a strained smile. "I'll be fine. But we need to get them out of here."

Every instinct screamed to argue, but Rodney was right. Whoever had fired hadn't gone far, and staying put made them sitting ducks. They needed someplace safe within a short few-hour hiking distance. But where?

Contemplating the answer, he rushed, grabbed their gear, and hurried back. It pained him to see Yolanda's face pale, and her arms locked tightly around Jenny in fear. Whatever was going on, nobody, let alone a mother and child, should ever have to go through something like this.

"Yolanda," he said gently. "Can you carry Jenny for a bit?" She nodded. "Good. Follow me."

He helped Rodney to his feet, pressing a firm hand against the wound as he took the role of crutch. Together, they moved deeper into the woods. Vincent knew a few spots nearby that could offer cover while they waited for authorities—but a single thought gnawed at him.

Why them?

This kind of violence didn't happen here. Not like this. Which meant there was a reason. Had they stumbled onto something? Was someone trying to keep a secret buried? Cartel? Corrupt officials? Or was it money—an inheritance, a spouse, a family dispute turned deadly?

Too many possibilities. No answers. Yet. And now, both his life and Rodney's were tangled up in it.

A little while later, they came to a dense cluster of boulders that they could rest behind for a moment. Needing to take care of Rodney's wound ASAP, he led them behind it. Easing him down, he carefully took a look at the wound.

"That's more than a graze," Vincent muttered, digging through his pack for the first-aid kit.

"Not by much," Rodney groaned as he shifted. "But yeah… you're right. I just knew we had to get them out before there were more shots."

"This is all my fault." They both looked up.

Rodney shook his head, wincing, "The only way any of this is your fault is if you ordered someone to shoot us. Otherwise, you and your daughter are victims under our protection."

"But I'm the one he's after."

"Rodney's right," Vincent added calmly as he worked. "None of this is your fault. But I *am* curious who would want to hurt you—and why."

Yolanda looked down at Jenny, who clutched her shirt and sobbed silently. Something dark coiled in Vincent's chest. He wanted to find the man behind this and bash his skull in. It was always bad enough when teens and adults did this to other teens and adults. But to a child that wasn't even a pre-teen!?

He wasn't a violent man. Most people would say he was too laid-back for his own good. But everyone had lines that others shouldn't cross. This was one of the rare few. Okay, the rare two.

Harming children was one. And hurting his people was the other. And today, both lines had been crossed. Yeah. He was furious.

With a shaking breath, Yolanda finally spoke. "My ex-husband. Though I don't know if that was him... or one of his goons."

"Why would he be after you?" Vincent asked quietly, keeping his tone steady as he cleaned the wound. He hoped she'd feel less pressured and continue to speak freely about it without feeling scrutinized.

"Because I found out about illegal things he was involved in. I was pregnant and terrified. So I went to the FBI and gave them what I found, begging them to protect my child and me from him. Next thing I know, they were whisking me away with a new identity."

Vincent's hands stilled. "You're in WITSEC!?" The words slipped out before he could stop them. The Witness Protection Program. A.K.A. WITSEC was a government program to protect those who were key witnesses against very dangerous people. And if they ever got found and disposed of... then those people had a higher chance of not being put behind bars, where they belonged.

What have we gotten ourselves involved in?

***

So much for an easy first day. Rodney groaned internally. He knew enough to understand what this meant. Yolanda and Jenny—whoever they truly were—would be whisked away again under new names, while he and Vincent would be told to keep quiet. *How* quiet, he didn't know.

"I thought we were finally safe," Yolanda said, her voice breaking as tears streamed down her face. "That's why I brought her here. I wanted her to experience what I loved every summer. I was such a fool."

"There's nothing wrong with wanting to share something that brought you joy," Rodney countered. "Yes, it was a risk. But if you hadn't seen hide nor hair of your ex and his lackeys, then it makes sense you'd think he'd probably stopped hunting you. Especially if we're nowhere near where you lived before with him."

Yolanda stared at him, eyes wide with stunned disbelief. A small, forgiving smile touched his face. Things like this happened—rarely, but they did. And while maybe she shouldn't have returned to a place tied so strongly to her past, he couldn't find it in himself to be angry.

Acadia was a natural beauty that mesmerized many visitors every year. Rodney had been one of them. He couldn't imagine ever being told he could never come back and bask in its natural wonders.

"Why don't we get you two somewhere safe," Vincent said softly, "and contact the Marshal in charge of your protection?"

Wiping her tears away, Yolanda nodded with quiet resolve. Rodney respected that. He knew situations like this broke people—and the fact that she was still standing strong spoke volumes.

They carefully got to their feet, scanning for any sign of movement. Nothing. Rodney should've felt relieved, but strangely, it only caused him to feel more unsettled. Fear of not knowing where this guy was? Maybe.

Feeling more unnerved by the second, Rodney glanced at his boss. "You got a spare gun?"

Vincent studied him. "Got a permit to use one?" He nodded and pulled his license from his pocket. His dad had insisted years ago. A *just-in-case* sort of thing.

Though a small handgun didn't really do much to a bear or a moose, it was better to have one than not. Especially if it's the only thing you have against an illegal poacher who'd rather shoot another in the woods than risk them going to the proper authorities. Rare as it was, it still happened from time to time—and it was part of why he wasn't more shaken about being shot.

After a moment, Vincent reluctantly shuffled through his bag. Pulling out another .40-caliber semi-automatic pistol and extra ammo, he handed it over.

"Thanks." Rodney tested the weight, then sobered. He knew from training and experience how dangerous guns were. One mistake could cost an innocent's life. Something he refused to have on his conscience if he could at all help it.

With a plan and destination in place, Vincent took point while Rodney covered their rear. Not ideal, given the pain gnawing at his side. But until they were safe, it was the only option. He only hoped that he'd spot the guy again before someone wound up more injured than him.

An hour of careful travel, and they had nearly gotten to the first section of the golf course up ahead without incident. Had they given up on the chase? Something in his gut screamed they weren't in the clear. So why hadn't they seen anyone?

Feeling more and more uneasy, he couldn't take it anymore. "Hold up!" They came to a halt as he scanned the area more thoroughly.

"You see something?"

After a moment or two, Rodney shook his head. "No. And that's the problem."

"Doesn't that just mean they're not following us?" Yolanda asked.

"He's hunted you for six years," Rodney said bluntly. "I doubt a little gunfire would've scared him off."

She frowned. "What are you—some kind of undercover agent?"

"I don't need a badge to recognize obsession," he snapped, then winced as pain flared. Drawing a careful breath, he continued, quieter. "I grew up in forests and learned how to survive in any condition. And thanks to that, I've developed a sort of danger sense."

"A danger sense? Isn't that what animals get?"

"People get them too," Vincent muttered. "Something tells me you've had reason to trust yours."

Rodney gave a confirming nod. "Though most of the time it was because of an aggressive bear or a moose heading my way. Rarely people. But it's going off like mad. And I doubt it's because of a testy animal."

"Then let's get to the Golf Course," Vincent urged.

Rodney shook his head. "I don't think that's a good idea."

"Why?"

"If they watched us from afar, then they could probably guess where we're headed and already set up a trap for us. So no. I think we should avoid this area altogether."

After a moment, Vincent gave a slow nod. "Then, how about we head to the Asticou Hotel? It's in the opposite direction."

"But I'm tired," Jenny whined.

Rodney crouched, forcing a smile despite the pain. "I know. We all are. How about this—we hike a bit more, then take a snack break. Okay?"

She pouted, then nodded. "Okay."

"That's my girl, Jenny." Rodney placed his hand on top of her head. "You know what? I think with how good a sport you're being, you deserve a cookie and chocolate milk when we get there. My treat. How does that sound?"

Her eyes lit up. "Really!?"

"You betcha."

"Yay!" A real smile slid up his face at her enthusiasm. Afterwards, they headed out.

A few hours and multiple stops later, they were nearing the hotel. And the long-awaited treat for the special little girl who was holding onto his hand at the moment. She wanted to get a piggyback ride, but his wound had made that impossible, so she had settled for this.

In truth, the pain had been getting worse as they went. And for the past hour, he'd been a bit light-headed and feeling heat under his skin. Fever, maybe. All signs that there might be more damage than he was letting on.

This is bad. He thought. But with the current situation, there was no way to deal with it.

He was smiling down at her, trying to keep his mind and worries on something other than his health, when Vincent's radio crackled. "Boss, do you read me? Over."

Unhooking it from his belt, Vincent answered. "This is Vincent. Go ahead, Rose."

"Is Rodney with you?"

Rodney took the radio. "I'm here. What's wrong, Rose?"

"The police are here. They need to speak with you. It's about your family."

His blood turned to ice. "My family? What happened?"

"Mr. Johnson," an unfamiliar voice said. "This is Officer Hills."

"Officer. What's happened? Are my parents okay? My brother?"

"There was a head-on collision."

"No." Rodney's heart sank to the pit of his stomach as Vincent took the radio back.

"This is Vincent Groober, Mr. Johnson's boss," Vincent said. "Where were they headed?"

"They had received a call about their son being wounded and needing them to come and convince him to be taken to the ER." Rodney felt his heart break as he lurched forward in the direction of the hotel, only to be stopped by Vincent's firm grip.

"Let me go!" Rodney cried out, ignoring the worsening pain from his injury.

"Not with you like this!" Vincent forced him back, grabbing his upper arms firmly as he continued to speak. "Rodney, listen to me! There's nothing you can do for them right now."

"They're my only family, Vincent! I need to be there for them."

"I understand. But what if this is the real trap? What if they found out who we are, and the call to your parents was made by them so they could use them to get what they want?"

Rodney froze as it dawned on him what he was saying. "Y-You think they..."

"Either they coerced someone into making the call, or they have someone amongst us that's on their side. And it's probably the one that brought them to this area."

"Casey!?" Rodney shook his head violently. "No. He wouldn't betray us. Not him."

"I don't think so either. At least not knowingly. The biggest question is how they would've gotten a hold of your parents anyway?"

The answer hit him like a ton of bricks. "I gave Casey my parents' home phone number for emergency purposes since we were almost always partnered up." The world felt like it was tilting as he fell to his knees, tears streaming down his face. "They have him."

Vincent's expression confirmed he had the same fear. But where was he now? Was he alright? Or was he out there, dying as his family might be? Or were they all...

He couldn't even finish that thought. If it were the truth, then he didn't think he'd be able to pull through. His parents and little brother were everything to him. And Casey was more than a fellow guide, but a mentor and friend.

He was beginning to feel like letting the encroaching darkness he'd been fighting come when Jenny threw her arms around him. Surprised, he didn't know what to do for a moment before wrapping his trembling arms around her.

"I'm so sorry, Rodney," Yolanda apologized.

"It's not your fault," He numbly replied.

"He's right." He could barely feel Vincent's comforting hand on his shoulder as the man softly spoke. "We need to get to the hotel and call the Marshal."

With a nod, Rodney got to his feet, and they made it to the Hotel. True to his word, he made sure Jenny got a cookie and chocolate milk, mostly to keep her distracted as Vincent and Yolanda called the Marshal in charge of them.

The next few days went by in a blur. After the Marshals and the FBI came and whisked Yolanda and Jenny away, Rodney and Vincent had to give their account of what happened. At least until Rodney had to be lifeflighted to the ER when he collapsed from an infection in his wound, lack of sleep, and lack of nutrition. He could barely remember what happened after that.

When he came to, he finished his recount to the FBI. After an hour, they got up to leave. But he needed to know something before they did.

"Before you go," Rodney looked up at them. "Have you heard if my parents and little brother survived the crash?"

Their expressions became shadowed as the one called Agent York spoke, "I'm sorry to have to tell you this. But I'm afraid they died on impact."

"No!" Something inside of him shattered. "No!" He barely acknowledged them, apologizing one more time before leaving. He had lost the only family he had left in this world. He was totally alone.

He didn't know how much time had passed before he felt comforting hands on him. Looking up, he was staring into the concerned faces of his two best friends. Gav Orben and Gage Linden.

"My family," Rodney gasped out between choked sobs. "They're gone."

With a pained nod, they carefully pulled him close as they let him fall apart in their arms.

***

Vincent was about to knock when the sound of Rodney's gut-wrenching cries stopped him cold. Had he just been told? Probably. What was he supposed to do? He didn't know him well enough to offer real comfort. Still... should he try anyway?

Deciding the answer was a yes, he took a deep breath and stepped inside. Immediately, he froze. Two young men were there, holding Rodney close—both of them familiar faces from past hikes. One had always complained about being outdoors, yet never once chose to wait in the car when offered the chance.

That one, Vincent had learned early on, was the son of a successful golfing businessman. From what Casey had told him, the man wasn't one to fall behind on any excursion—he just didn't like being in nature. And right now, he was staring straight at Vincent.

After a moment, the young man—Gage, if Vincent remembered correctly—leaned down and whispered something to the other. When the second man—*Gav?*—glanced toward Vincent, he gave a short nod. Gage stood and approached, gently ushering Vincent back into the hallway.

Leaning against the wall, Gage fixed him with a hard stare. "What happened out there? And don't tell me he was too stubborn to get medical help. I know Rodney well enough to know that's not true."

"I imagine you do," Vincent said, shaking his head, frustration and grief twisting together. "But I'm afraid I can't talk about it. And neither can he."

Gage's jaw tightened. "Does it have anything to do with the FBI talking to him?" Vincent looked away, saying nothing.

"I see." Gage exhaled slowly. "Then I won't pry. But I'm gonna be frank with you—people are starting to think that the reason he wasn't there right away is that he had a hand in his family's death."

"What!?" Vincent snapped, disbelief flooding his face. "No. He loved them more than anyone could imagine. He'd never do that. We were too busy running for our lives—" He stopped himself, realizing he'd already said too much.

"I'm glad you see that too," Gage said, relief breaking through his anger. "Though I don't like the fact that you two were running for your lives—and even less that you can't tell me from whom—but as I said, I won't pry."

Vincent let out a slow breath. "Thanks. I know it's probably best to let you guys help him. I won't get in the way. But… I wanted him to know Casey's still alive. He was beaten pretty badly, though."

Gage reeled back. "Casey!? You mean whoever did this forced him to call them?"

"He accidentally said Rodney's last name when they described who'd been shot," Vincent replied quietly. "They beat him, trying to get more information. When that didn't work, they took his phone and found his parents' number."

"So that's how this happened."

Vincent nodded, pain heavy in his chest. "Casey's beside himself. He blames himself for everything. I don't know if having him around will help distract Rodney while he heals—but he deserves to know the truth."

"I agree," Gage said, regaining his composure. "But I'll be honest with you, Mr. Groober—I doubt Rodney will be able to pull himself back up for years."

Vincent stiffened as Gage continued. "The Johnsons were a tight-knit unit. Unbreakable. They had no one else, so they looked after each other. Even their list of friends was small—small enough to fit on a single page of a palm-sized notebook."

"That's hard to believe," Vincent murmured. "If they were all anything like Rodney, I'd figure they'd have loads of friends. So why don't they?"

"Because they valued *true* friendships," Gage said. "The kind that lasts through just about anything. Casey is one of those people—to Rodney. And to me."

He turned toward the door but hesitated. "If you want, I can tell him. But…" He glanced back. "I think it would be better if he heard it from you."

Without another word, the young man walked in, leaving Vincent to stare, dumbfoundedly, at the closed door. Should he tell him? After a moment, he followed.

For the next few years, Gage's prediction proved painfully accurate. Rodney sank into a deep depression—one many believed he would never escape... That is, until the birth of his beloved daughter.

The End

The Veiled Path

Short Story 2

The Veiled Path

Filling out his usual Search and Rescue (SAR) report, Rodney Johnson's fingers continued to fly over the keyboard. Though most of the time, he was having fun out there guiding or rescuing people, it wasn't the only part of his job. And right now, with no scheduled guides and no calls yet for another rescue, he was stuck at his desk doing them. It beat twiddling his thumbs. Barely.

With the final bit typed up, he saved and sent it in. Relieved to finally be done, he leaned back, hands behind his head, with a sigh. As usual, it was a pain writing up the reports. But what was he to do? Pawn it off to someone who wasn't there and hope they got something right? That'd be a great way to get fired.

Gage had suggested bringing a handheld game for slow days like this. The only thing was, Rodney didn't own one and never planned to since he wasn't big on games, nor watching TV. He did enjoy the occasional board game and cards, but that was the extent of it.

He did have a hobby outside of climbing mountains and hiking through the woods: cooking. Yeah, he enjoyed cooking whatever dish he had the ingredients for. The only thing was, they had all eaten a little over an hour ago and were still pretty satisfied. So cooking anything would be a waste of ingredients. But maybe not for hot cocoa...

"All done?"

Looking up, he smiled at his boss and good friend, Vincent Groober. "Just finished. And hopefully, won't need to fill out another one for a while."

"I don't blame you," Vincent scoffed. "If you ask me, paperwork's the true menace of society."

Rodney chuckled. "You said it." That was one of the many things he liked about his boss. They thought much alike. They both loved being out in nature and hated being stuck with desk duty.

"Though I can't help but ask, was it *really* a bear he was being chased by?"

"More like a mountain of a man wearing a fur coat that was trying to warn him about the territorial moose up ahead. But I could understand why he thought that. What with him sounding more grrish behind that thick ski mask and all."

"Hmph. People these days."

Rodney couldn't agree more. Thanks to Mr. Taylor a.k.a. Bear Man, who was unwilling to lower his mask to be clearly heard, Mr. Millard had gotten spooked and took a tumble into a creek. Fortunately, Mr. Taylor had pulled him out and kept him warm as they came to his rescue. He had to say, it had been one of the weirdest calls he'd ever taken.

He was about to explain all that when the radio squawked with an unfamiliar voice. "Mayday! Mayday! Can anyone hear me? Over."

Snatching up the radio as the man finished the last word, Rodney quickly responded. "This is Rodney Johnson with the Search and Rescue Team. I hear you loud and clear. What's your emergency? Over."

"I injured my leg, and I can't walk on it. I think it might be broken. I need assistance right away."

No kidding. With temperatures in the low forties, staying still for too long was an open invitation to hypothermia. There was no time to waste.

"What's your name?"

"Tony. Tony Barns."

"Alright, Mr. Barns. I need you to tell me where you are so we can get to you as quickly as possible."

"I'm on top of Pemetic Mountain."

Pemetic Mountain, huh? He had hoped it would be in the more wind-protected areas for his sake.

"Alright. Hang in there, Mr. Barns. We'll get you down as soon as we can. In the meantime, do everything you can to stay warm. Over and out."

Setting down the radio, he was about to jump to his feet and call out the emergency when he was startled to hear Rose Brandy call out a different emergency. "We've got an emergency! A little girl strayed away from her parents on the Norumbega Mountain Loop."

"We've also got a lost family near the Jordan Ponds," Chase Wells called out next.

"Looks like we've got three emergencies," Vincent grumbled.

Finally able to speak up, Rodney jumped to his feet and called out his emergency. "A hiker had injured, possibly broken, his leg on top of Pemetic Mountain."

"Three different calls and only five of us can leave to help," Lucas Patterson groaned.

"Everyone," Vincent called out, taking command of the situation. "Gather for a strategy meeting. Casey? Call Brandon. We're going to need an air rescue for the downed hiker."

Pushing together the two tables and bringing over the map, they all loomed over it as Casey Randle placed the phone near it. "Alright, Brandon. We're all here, and we've got a big issue."

"What's the emergency?" Brandon demanded.

"We've got three of them," Vincent replied. "One is for a hiker with a possible broken leg on top of Pemetic Mountain."

They heard him breathe in through his teeth. "That's not good. Unfortunately, I won't be able to get there right away. I'm life-flighting someone to the Hospital and have no time or room to swing by at the moment."

"How long will it take you?"

"If everything goes well... an hour and a half, tops."

"Then we have no choice but to send someone ahead of you. Rodney?" Vincent looked up at him. "Get to Mr. Barns and stabilize that leg. Brandon will meet you there just as soon as he can. And whatever you do, stay in constant radio contact."

With a determined nod, Rodney replied, "Will do." With that, he quickly grabbed his gear and headed out the door.

He was nearly to one of the vehicles when he heard someone calling from behind. "Wait up!" Chase and Lucas came running over as Rose and Casey jumped into a different one. "We'll drop you off since we're in the vicinity."

"Sounds good to me." Hopping into the back, Rodney buckled up as the other two did the same. Before he knew it, they were speeding down the road to their destination. And he meant speeding.

A sharp turn nearly pulled a yelp out of him. Was he gonna make it there in one piece? "Chase!" He snapped. "Slow down before you kill us."

"Relax," Chase complacently spoke. "I do this all the time, and I've not once gotten into a wreck." Rodney groaned his displeasure. Sure, Chase was a great guide and rescuer, but he always had too much of a childish side. Boy, was he glad seatbelts were invented.

Once there, he grumbled a quick thanks as he jumped out with his things. Glad to be out of the death trap and on solid ground, he slipped on his gear and headed up the mountain. He knew every moment counted if he wanted to help Mr. Barns before he got hypothermia in this temperature. He only hoped the man had an emergency blanket and hand warmers.

For roughly thirty minutes, he hiked up as Casey's voice came on, letting them know that he and Rose had found the missing family and were guiding them out. Apparently, they had decided to go off-trail to follow a fox and couldn't find their way back. Not long after, he was relieved to hear that Chase and Lucas had found the missing girl. After a quick congratulations and update on his location, he continued.

Roughly twenty minutes before making it to the top, where he saw someone wrapped in an emergency blanket. "Mr. Barns?" With his attention, Rodney made his way over. "I'm Rodney Johnson from the Search and Rescue Team."

"Oh, thank goodness," Tony sighed in relief as he looked in the direction Rodney came from. "Where's the rest of your team?"

"On other emergency calls at the moment." He quickly spoke up as he focused on the unbent leg. "But don't worry. We have a helicopter heading our way as soon as he's done with his current emergency."

"How long will that take?"

"Thirty minutes tops. Then we can get you out of here." With a thorough assessment, Rodney dug into his backpack. "Looks like your assumption's probably right. I'll have to stabilize it for an easier airlift."

Getting to work, he carefully stabilized the leg and then readied for an easy airlift. As he finished, a faint noise carried on the wind. Turning toward it, relief washed over him at the sight of the familiar rescue helicopter cresting the ridge. Earlier than predicted.

"Looks like he overestimated his time," he said with a smirk toward the injured man. "Looks like in five minutes, you'll be on your way to the hospital."

Tony sighed. "I'd rather him overestimate rather than under. I can't wait to get home and-" The words died as a sudden gust of icy wind slammed into them from the side, sharp enough to steal the breath from his lungs and nearly knock them over.

Rodney threw up an arm to shield his face and turned into the wind. The sky was changing. Where moments ago it had been clear, a thick, dark mass was churning into existence —swirling, spreading, pressing low. Nimbostratus. A storm cloud. And it hadn't rolled in from the horizon. It was forming *right* beside the mountain.

That's not possible. His stomach dropped as the wind intensified, biting through layers, carrying the promise of snow. This was already bad—worsening by the second—and catastrophic for an air rescue.

Snapping his attention back to the helicopter, his heart lurched as it wobbled midair, pivoting hard before banking away. Tearing his radio free, Rodney called out in concern, "Brandon, do you copy? Are you alright? Over."

"Affirmative," Brandon replied, his voice tight with strain. "But if I don't land this bird now, I won't be. I'm sorry, Rodney."

"Don't be. Get to safety. I'll figure something out."

But what? He had been expecting a flight back to the station. Now with the wind rising fast, visibility already beginning to smear, and the only shelter anywhere near them was the boulder field. They were running out of options.

The radio squawked, his boss' voice cutting through the wind. "Can you and Mr. Barns hunker down someplace, Rodney? Over?"

He drew breath to answer—but the wind surged harder, slamming into them from the side. Instinctively, he shifted his body to shield Tony, taking the brunt of it himself. This was getting too dangerous. And the only real shelter was miles downslope, beyond a steep, exposed descent.

Rodney pulled the radio close and shouted, "Negative. I'm taking Mr. Barns down to the Jordan Pond House. Over."

"That's suicide!" Casey's voice snapped, fear bleeding through his usually ironclad tone. "Find a place to hunker down and wait for help."

"Where!?" Rodney shot back. "The boulder fields? In these winds, that's just as big a risk- if not bigger."

"Find a crevice and pitch up a barrier-"

"It'd be torn to shreds in minutes," Rodney cut in. "We have to get off the mountain and into the trees for any chance at all. If the temperature keeps dropping, we'll freeze before anyone reaches us. Casey… we don't have a choice. We move, or we die."

There was a brief crackle of silence.

"How strong are the winds up there?" Rose's voice came through, tight with concern.

"Strong enough that I have to crawl if I don't want to be swept off my feet. And worse- I can't tell which direction it's coming from anymore."

The wind had become chaotic, striking from all sides at once. Not gusts—*pressure*. As if they were standing inside the storm itself. Something he'd never experienced before. And he knew it was going to get worse.

"It's your call, Rodney," Vincent deadpanned. "But it sounds like your window's closing fast." Looking at Tony, he knew from the terror in the man's eyes that he had only one option.

"We'll head to the restaurant," Rodney explained. "We'll cut through the trees and follow Jordan Pond up in. If conditions change, I'll build a shelter, and we'll hunker down and hope the storm breaks by nightfall."

He knew that was the coin toss. If they had to stop, their odds dropped sharply. The temperature had started in the forties —and it was falling far too fast. By nightfall, it could be well below zero. With limited gear and only a few hours of retained heat, seven hours might as well have been eternity.

"Alright," Vincent replied, his voice already starting to break up. "Stay safe."

"Roger," Rodney responded. "Over and out."

We're what!? Staring in terrified disbelief, Tony couldn't believe what he just heard. They were going to hike through *this!*? It wasn't safe- especially not in his condition.

"How are we getting down with my leg broken?" he cried.

"Carefully. Together." Rodney met his gaze with stark determination. "Trust me. If there were a safer option, we'd be taking it- especially with that leg."

"But I can't put pressure on it."

"I know. That's why I'll be your crutch. And if there's any point I have to carry you, then I will. But we have to do this if we're going to get back to the people who care about us."

He means it.

Tony's eyes widened at the raw honesty in the man's voice. Rodney had a goal, and he wasn't letting fear dictate his actions. Unlike Tony himself.

With a small nod, he followed Rodney's step-by-step instructions as snow began to fall in earnest.

***

After making sure the ladder into the boulder field was secure, Rodney helped Tony down. Every step was slow and painful. With no strength in his injured leg, they had to move even more carefully to get to safety.

Once down, Rodney slung Tony's arm over his shoulders, taking a good portion of the man's weight. They needed to get out of the area before things got too risky. They had just passed a cluster of boulders when a chilling sound echoed from behind them. Whipping his head around, his eyes widened as several loose rocks came tumbling toward them.

"GET DOWN!" he shouted, releasing Tony and throwing himself over him as they ducked behind the boulder cluster. He squeezed his eyes shut, praying his pack wouldn't get snagged by one of the rocks and drag him down. Because if that happened, he might become more of a liability instead of help.

A long minute passed with only one noticeable, but not dangerously hard, tug from a boulder grazing the top of his backpack before the rest finally settled. Shaken by the near miss, Rodney carefully lifted his head and looked for any more immediate dangers. Fortunately, there wasn't any. At least for now.

Swallowing, he got up and helped Tony to his feet. "Let's move before more comes our way."
Tony's body trembled, his face pale with fear. There was no time to stop and calm him. Too many people panicked in situa-

tions like this. Rodney pressed on, grateful that Tony followed without resistance.

Not more than thirty minutes later, a thick fog rolled in, reducing the visibility to barely a foot in front of them. With it came a deeper, sharper cold, making him even more grateful for the warmers he packed. Under normal conditions, they'd last hours—but this storm wasn't normal.

On average, the hike down took him roughly forty minutes. At their pace, it would be at least twice that—still within the window. The problem was the cold. It made everything sluggish. Heavy. Wrong.

Sometime after reaching a shallow incline, Rodney couldn't feel the warmth of the heaters anymore. Fear prickled at him as he tightened his grip on Tony and pushed onward. As long as he hadn't made a wrong turn, they were close to Jordan Pond. And once they reached it, all they had to do was follow the shoreline to the restaurant nestled against it.

Cold and shivering, they walked for a while longer over ground that soon became... flat. Too flat. Coming to a halt, he looked around as confusion spiked in his senses. He didn't remember an area like this anywhere nearby.

So where— A sharp cracking sound split the silence beneath his feet. Understanding hit him like a sucker punch out of nowhere. He was standing *on* Jordan Pond.

Realizing his mistake a bit too late, Rodney shoved Tony back as the ice gave way, plunging him into shockingly cold water.

***

Oomf. Falling onto his back with a grunt, Tony scrambled to sit up as he heard the splash. Breathing heavily from fear, he looked out, hoping he was wrong. Rodney was gone.

This can't be happening!

"Rodney!" he cried, dropping onto his stomach and dragging himself as close to the broken edge as he dared. He peered in, but aside from the ripples left behind, he saw nothing. Where was he? "Rodney!"

As panic began to take hold, Tony noticed something—a shadow moving beneath the surface. As he realized what it was, Rodney broke through the water with a violent gasp. He was alive.

"Rodney!" He held out his hand as the SAR member turned toward him. Without hesitation, Rodney grabbed it. Within moments, Tony hauled him out, and together they dragged themselves far enough away to be sure they were back on solid ground.

Tony tore open an emergency blanket and wrapped it tightly around Rodney. Though he feared it would do little good now.

Teeth chattering, Rodney attempted a smile. "Th-th-thanks."

"Thank me after we make it out," Tony said firmly, gripping his shoulder through the crinkling foil. "Is this Jordan Pond?"

"Y-yes. W-we n-need t-to head s-s-south f-from h-here."

"Which way's south?" Rodney pointed, his hand shaking. Tony studied him, worry etched across his face. "You think you can stand?"

He gave a small nod. "F-for n-now at l-least." Without another word, Rodney grabbed Tony's arm and hauled him upright, just as he had before the plunge. Tony was relieved he still had the strength—but for how long?

They walked for what felt like forever before Rodney's pace slowed. Tony's attention snapped to him—and his stomach dropped. Rodney was no longer shivering. His skin had gone pale, his eyes dulled by exhaustion. Even his grip had weakened.

There was no question as to why. Hypothermia was taking hold. They needed to find the House. Now.

"R-Rodney?" Tony rasped.

"We need to find you a temporary crutch," Rodney said sluggishly.

"What?" Tony faltered. "A-Am I getting t-too h-heavy for y-you?"

"My body's getting too weak to keep you upright. I don't think I'll make it if I continue. Actually..." His voice dropped. "I'm starting to wonder if I'm going to make it at all."

This can't be happening!

"D-Don't t-talk like that!" Tony shook his head. "Y-You can't g-give up. W-Where almost th-there."

"I'm not," Rodney replied softly. "I'm just... preparing you for if- or when- you have to leave me behind."

"Stop it!" Tony snapped. "Y-You can't talk like that, or y-you might as well be t-tossing in the towel. After all you've d-done for me... Y-You can't die b-because of m-me."

"If I die," Rodney countered, tiredly meeting his eyes, "it won't be because of you. It'd be the fault of the storm. And me... for not realizing we were standing on the pond." His voice softened. "So please. Let me do this for you."

Tony's chest ached as he nodded. The thought of Rodney freezing to death was unbearable—but the storm had only worsened since the fall.

Will this nightmare ever end?

Stopping underneath a stand of trees, Rodney moved closer to one. "Wait here while I look." Without a word, he obliged, leaning heavily against the trunk for support.

Concerned by Rodney's unsteady sway, Tony grabbed his arm. "Hey. W-while you're l-looking for something for m-me, find s-something for yourself t-too. Got it?" He knew it wouldn't help when the man's body finally succumbed to the bitter cold, but he hoped that it would slow the process down. Perhaps buy him a bit more time.

After a moment, Rodney nodded and began searching. Tony didn't know if anything could be found under all the snow, but the man was determined. He watched, forcing himself not to intervene, no matter how painful it was.

In truth, Tony was beginning to doubt whether either of them would survive. He didn't know the area as well as the experienced SAR rescuer. And if Rodney collapsed too soon...

After a couple of minutes, Rodney returned with two thick enough branches and handed him one shaped like a crude Y. "Here. This should work."

"T-thanks." Tony tested it. "Rodney? W-where do we go from h-here?"

"Normally, taking this path would be best." Rodney paused. "But I think cutting through the woods would be faster. It'll take us to the parking lot. From there... the House Restaurant." With a nod, they pressed on.

Time blurred as Tony's shivering slowed and his energy faded. The pain in his broken leg was gone too—something he would've been grateful for if he didn't know what it meant. They had to get to the House Restaurant. Fast.

Moments later, they were no longer surrounded by trees, and the ground leveled beneath their feet. Was this the parking lot Rodney mentioned? It was hard to tell with the dense fog and snow swirling around them. It didn't take long before they came across snow-covered vehicles.

He wanted to leap for joy, but his weakened state prevented it. A moment later, something larger loomed ahead. Not a building—but bigger than a car. A helicopter. Its frame was intact, coated in snow and ice.

"Looks like..." Rodney tiredly spoke. "Brandon... landed... safely."

"Which means we'll be airlifted to the hospital as soon as this storm lets up," Tony encouraged. "Come on. We're almost there. Which way to the building?"

Fear clutched his chest as confusion crossed Rodney's face. "The... building?"

"The Jordan Pond House Restaurant? You're leading us there, remember?"

"House restaurant... yes. I remember. It's close."

Moving in a near zombie-like haze, Rodney passed the helicopter and continued on. Tony hesitated, uncertain which way—or how far from the parking lot it might be—then followed slowly. When the trees closed in again, doubt crept in, but he said nothing.

Trying to keep Rodney's spirits up, Tony spoke words of encouragement as they hobbled along. He was relieved to get a grunt or slight nod at first, but when Rodney's pace continued to slow—and then he stopped responding altogether—his worry deepened. Where was that dang restaurant?

Tony was beginning to doubt they were heading in the right direction when a faint glow caught his attention. Was it... Yes, it was! The restaurant was only feet away.

"See, Rodney?" Tony said brightly, forcing hope into his voice. "We're almost there. Just a few more steps and we'll be able to warm up." His smile faltered when Rodney didn't even try to acknowledge that he heard him. He was running out of time.

Every step closer to the promise of warmth fueled the next. He couldn't wait to sit by the fire and chase away this cold that was trying to lull him into a forever sleep. He wasn't going to let it win. Not now. Not ever.

He nearly cried for joy as the door came into full view. "Rodney, look—" The words died in his throat as he helplessly watched Rodney collapse into the snow.

"Rodney!" Tony cried, dropping to his knees beside him, shaking his shoulder. "Rodney! Come on! You can't give up. We're almost there."

A low groan and a slight movement from Rodney's head were all he got. Fear lodged in his throat. Rodney was going to die unless he did something. And as much as he didn't want to leave him out there, Tony knew he needed to get him help.

Scrambling to his feet, he hastily limped to the door. Pulling it open, he cried out. "HELP! PLEASE!" Several employees rushed toward him, but Tony waved them off desperately. "No—not me. Rodney Johnson. He collapsed out there." One of them stayed to help him as the others bolted outside.

"Sir, please," the man gently spoke. "Come with me." Tony nodded numbly and let himself be led away.

***

Hours had come and gone since they were taken into the off-site employee dormitory, where Tony hadn't seen hide nor hair of anyone since he was taken care of. Not surprising, since most of their time had gone into saving Rodney's life. When they had brought him in...

He shivered at the thought of his unmoving form. Though he knew Rodney was still breathing at the time, he couldn't help but fear that they had gotten here too late. He had lost the will to continue mere seconds before walking through that door. *Seconds.*

Though he was grateful it happened so close to the building, where someone could reach him quickly. Still, it didn't stop his mind from replaying that awful scene. He didn't know if he'd ever get over it.

Trying to shake that memory, he heard the sound of a door closing. Glancing over, he realized it was the SAR Pilot, Brandon Riley, emerging from the room where Rodney had been placed.

"Is he okay?" Tony asked as the man walked over.

"He's alive, at least," Brandon sighed, sliding into the chair opposite him. "How about you? Holding up okay?"

"Thanks to Rodney," Tony stiffly shrugged. "But never mind me. Has he woken up?"

"I'm afraid not." Brandon's expression became shadowed. "And unless he does, or his body temperature finally rises..."

His body temperature still hadn't... Tony felt a lump form in his throat. He knew that was a bad sign. But until the storm blew over, there wasn't much they could do.

"Mr. Barns." Brandon leaned forward. "Could you please tell me everything that happened out there?" Hesitantly, he obliged. Though most of it was easy enough to go over, the others choked him up. He'd have to pause for a breath or two before pushing through.

By the end, Brandon leaned back, shaking his head in disbelief. "Even after falling in the Pond, he made it here. If it were anyone else who did, I'd be doubting your story."

"Look, I know it sounds crazy," Tony said firmly, "but it's the truth. He stayed calm and brought me here."

"I believe you. Rodney's always had a strong will that rarely breaks, and enough determination to lead an army. If anyone could do what you described, it would definitely be him. I'd

also say Casey and Vincent, but they've gotten a bit too sensi-
tive to cold weather in their older years."

"I see."

"I doubt it," Brandon scoffed before his attention drifted
to Tony's leg. "Can I take a look?" With a nod, he looked back
at the roaring fireplace. He already had little hope for his leg.

With every question Tony answered, the more he was
certain his leg was a goner. It was all due to carelessly looking
anywhere but where he was walking... and that freak storm. And
as much as the thought of losing it was a difficult pill to swal-
low, at least he was still alive. Thanks to the man who was cur-
rently fighting for his life.

He gave a heavy sigh. "What are the odds of getting a
prosthetic leg?"

"If you wind up losing your real one..." Brandon held up
a hand to halt any argument that was about to come. "I can't actually say whether you will or won't, no matter what I think.
But if that does happen, then the odds are in your favor."

"I'm being serious."

"So am I. I only have a basic medical degree. I can't
promise what will happen, only do what I can to keep you alive
—and save your leg if possible. Even if it seems hopeless.
That's my job."

Tony shook his head in frustration. "I don't know how
you do a job like that. If it were me, I'd have quit already."

"That's because you're only looking at the negative.
Sure, I fly people to the hospital—but most survive because I
got them there in time."

"But what about the ones that you couldn't save? How
do you handle those?"

"I admit that those times are tough," Brandon stiffly
shrugged. "I've questioned whether or not there was something

I could've done differently. Or if I'd been able to get there a few minutes sooner... maybe things would've turned out different. Like earlier."

Tony reeled back in surprise. "But you were on another call."

"I had stopped to fuel up before coming. I always do that when I'm below a quarter tank. But it wasted ten minutes that could've been used to save you both."

"Would it have been enough?"

"Possibly. But I'd be running on fumes after dropping you off."

"Then you made the right call. Actually, it's good to know that it's all fueled up for when the storm ends to get Rodney out of here."

"Something that wouldn't have mattered if you two had hunkered down somewhere like Casey had advised."

Tony couldn't believe what he was hearing. "Rodney made the decision he felt was right."

"That may be true, but it was a huge risk to take. And now look at him."

"He's a professional Search and Rescuer. If there was another way, I'm positive he would've done it."

Brandon's eyes narrowed. "I hope you're willing to say that against anyone who might try to use this incident against him or those who supported his decision."

"Against!?" Tony blinked. "Who would be against him?"

"This was an incident with no warning—a lone SAR rescuing a downed hiker. Anyone craving a juicy story—or with a beef against the team—would twist it, label it reckless. That would hurt all our positions. Possibly ruin our lives."

"Ridiculous!" Tony barked. "Rodney saved my life repeatedly. He stayed composed when I panicked and took command. He's a rescuer through and through. One I'd gladly stand up for."

"Hey, I'm on his side, remember?" Brandon replied, putting his hands up in mock surrender. "But plenty would argue he should have taken Casey's advice and sheltered in a ravine."

"If it were a normal storm, then I'd agree. But with how we were being slammed from all around us, I doubt we would've walked out of there without being squished. Those winds were perilous. And as I said before, rocks were being tossed at us when we were getting through the boulder field.

"Even when we were in the shelter of the trees. It was bad, but manageable enough to walk upright. And even then, we had to be careful about branches falling on top of us. This place was our *only* option. Especially since we didn't have enough warmers to last through the night."

A shudder wracked his body as the memory of Rodney collapsing replayed. He knew he'd never fully get over it. The SAR had risked his life for Tony's and never let any fear take over. Not even after falling into the pond.

"I'll bet that's one of the biggest reasons he made that call." His attention snapped back to Brandon as the man gave a sad, humorless laugh. "He sees and somehow senses the dangers ahead and calculates the best way to get around them. Even if it seems risky."

Tony gave an understanding nod. "He did that the whole time. Always aware of his surroundings and never giving up. Like cutting through the woods to get to the parking lot instead of following the path. I think... I think he knew that it was his only chance to survive."

"I wouldn't be surprised. There would also be more areas not protected by trees if you guys had followed the path. Which would mean more battering from the wind and speeding up the hypothermia for both of you."

Tony fell silent, reflecting on that. "You said he *senses* danger. How?"

"I wish I knew," Brandon scoffed, leaning back. "All I know is that he does. If you ask him, he'd claim that it's because his Dad used to take him out into the forest since before he could walk. But if you ask anyone in Ellsworth, they'll scoff at the idea and refuse to speculate, and urge you not to snoop any further. Even the news reports and gossipers clam up."

"Even them!?"

Brandon nodded solemnly. "Everything's on the hush-hush around there. Something catastrophic must have happened to him. I think everyone's just trying to protect him from it. Rodney's a good guy that everyone there seems to admire."

With a slow nod, Tony looked back into the crackling fireplace. He was curious about what could've happened. But he respected Rodney too much to pry. So whatever happened was going to remain unknown... at least to him.

***

Four days had passed since the incident, and Rodney was typing away at the report. Having been stuck in the hospital since he was lifeflighted two days prior, he was ready to get out of there. But because of how close he had gotten to dying, the doctor refused to let him go yet.

He supposed he couldn't blame him. What with needing to be on that dang bypass machine before he could fully pull through. And Tony... well, he was sad to hear he had lost his leg, the strain and brutal cold having done too much damage.

Finishing the report, Rodney heard a knock on his hospital room door. "It's open!"

Vincent walked in with a smirk as he noticed the laptop. "That bored, huh?"

"Better believe it," Rodney chuckled. "But I shouldn't be in an hour or so."

"So I've heard." Vincent pulled a chair close and sat down, all joking now gone from his face. "How do you feel?"

"Good, with all things considered." Rodney's smile disappeared as he looked down at his hands. "But Doc said I probably won't be able to handle the cold as well as I used to." The thought still unsettled him.

"So you might need to... avoid rescues during the winter months?"

"Oh, no." He quickly spoke up. "He didn't say anything like that. Just to dress warmer. That's all."

"That's good to hear. But I'm worried about your mental state. Will you be able to *mentally* handle it? You did almost die."

"Good question." Rodney thought for a moment before giving a nonchalant shrug. "I guess we won't know until I'm back out there. But I'd like to make sure I'm partnered with someone for a while, even if it's rescuing on one of the easy loops."

Vincent gave a relaxed smile. "I can understand that. Anything else?"

"One." Rodney took a deep breath before plowing through. "I need answers to what happened back there. That storm... it was like nothing I've ever witnessed before."

"I know what you mean." Vincent's expression turned grim. "But before I tell you what I know, tell me if anything struck you as odd about any animals you saw out there."

"That's the thing. The animals were acting as if nothing was coming. No storm. No danger. Nothing. And the weirdest part..."

Rodney turned away, hesitant to say the next part. He knew he was going to, but would Vincent think him crazy? Probably.

"I'm listening, Rodney," Vincent encouraged.

"The way the storm moved," Rodney carefully explained. "It seemed to have started roughly a mile away from Pemetic and swirled together like nothing I've ever seen. Like it was... made. Not formed."

An uncomfortable silence filled the room. He knew what he had said wasn't possible. And yet... that's the way it had felt.

"Is that your honest opinion?"

Rodney gave a small nod before facing Vincent. "Look, I know what I just said isn't possible. But with the sudden wind speed and the unnatural change from clear blue sky to... that!? I just... I just don't know how else that could be possible."

Vincent gave an understanding nod. "Then we've got to check the area beneath where it formed."

Rodney's eyes grew wide in surprise. "You believe me?"

"You're right about it not being natural. Which is why I've already checked every resource I could to see how this could've happened."

"Nothing?"

"Not unless you believe magic exists. And quite frankly, I don't. I only believe in Nature and science."

"Same." Rodney gave a relieved breath. "I want to see if we can find whatever idiotic device was used to cause this."

"And hope the idiot's still alive to make he or she pay for what they've done."

A couple of days later, they finally could get to the area... and they had found only a frozen corpse. No devices. And no indication of anything else being there.

The End

The Enigmatic Pickpocket

Short Story 3

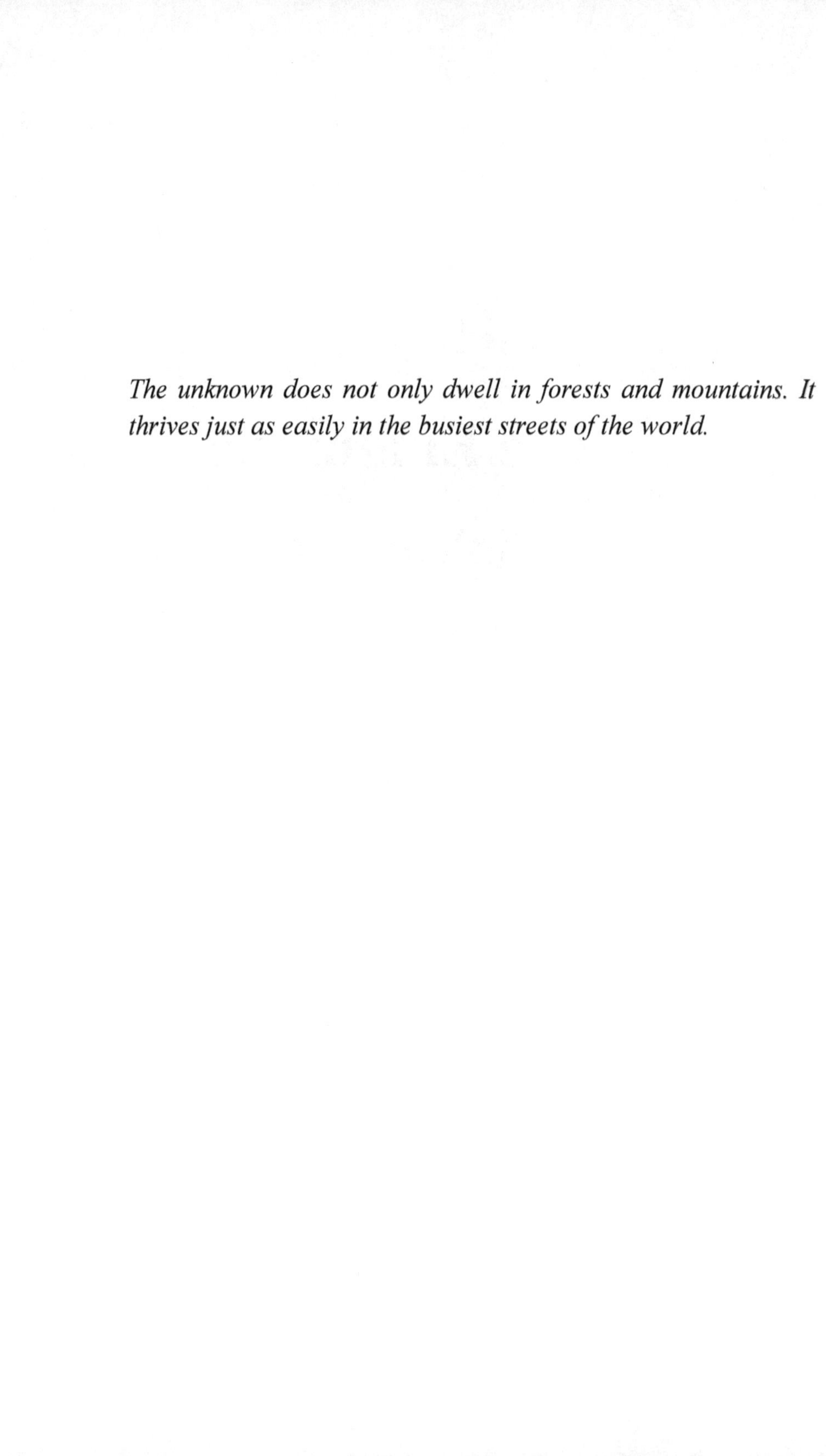

The unknown does not only dwell in forests and mountains. It thrives just as easily in the busiest streets of the world.

The Enigmatic Pickpocket

At last!

Walking at a leisurely pace, Special Agent Kirk Kline was enjoying his long-awaited vacation in Rome, Italy. A place where buildings of the past and present stood side by side. A wonderful place to visit... as long as you don't mind the high traffic.

Sidestepping another distracted walker, he chuckled. Yeah, he was one of those crazy fools. If his partner were here, he would find it bothersome. But not Kirk. He saw it as a fun way to keep on his toes.

But that wasn't the reason why he had left his hotel room this morning. He wanted to find the perfect present for his partner's only son. After all, a kid only turned nine once, and he was quite the little rascal, especially for the youngster's mother, who had her hands full with him. But before the searching commenced...

Turning the corner, he got a good whiff of the delicious aroma of what he was after. Following his nose into the Riscioli Caffe, he looked around. As it had been each time he visited, the brightly lit place was packed. No surprise when their coffees and sweet treats were the best all around.

A good fifteen minutes later, he was walking out with a cup of iced coffee and his favorite treat. Taking a bite of the Crostata Ricotta E Visciole Pastry, he groaned in delight. The sour cherry jam, layered with the sweet ricotta cream, felt like the harmonious flavors were tap dancing on his taste buds. Pair that with his Iced Latte... he was in heaven.

Although when he was undercover or in headquarters, Kirk tended to drink straight black coffee. Mostly not to stand out. The other reason was to not be distracted by his past.

Without fail, whenever he had an iced latte, he always thought of his late wife. It was her favorite drink. Actually, anything sweet was her favorite. He tried to limit her sweet intake when they were in financial trouble... but that fierce little spitfire wouldn't have it. She made sure he had plenty of work to keep the sweets coming.

It hadn't been hard when she was his secretary for the Investigative Business he owned back then. It had become a successful one with plenty of clients. At least, until he decided that he was done with that kind of work. His wife was glad about that, up until she drew her last breath after jumping in the way of an attack that was meant for him.

After many years, he needed to do something before his broken heart left him as an empty shell. And just like that, he had become an agent. The job saved him from self-wallowing. But what really began to heal him was his unbelievable partner. He owed him his life.

Enjoying the wonderful trip down memory lane as he took the last bite of his pastry, he didn't notice the kid until he bumped into him. Snapped back to the present, he glanced down at the boy, who looked roughly around his partner's son's age.

"Oh, excuse me," The boy apologized as he began to quickly move around him. Kirk was about to shrug it off when something caught his eye. The boy was slipping something familiar into his little pocket. His wallet.

Grabbing the boy's thin wrist, Kirk said sharply, "Hold it, kid."

"Hey! Let go!" The boy tried to pull his arm away to no avail. "Please, Mister. I said I was sorry."

He was impressed with the kid. Though he was clearly afraid, he held his ground. Not many criminals of any age could do that when caught. Maybe this firm lesson would straighten him out before he fell any deeper down that rabbit hole.

"Easy, kid," Kirk carefully spoke. "I'm not gonna hurt you. However, I would like you to return what you stole from me. After that, how about you and I find a place to chat about this pickpocketing lifestyle you picked up?"

The boy's eyes grew wide as his face paled. The fear coming off him was understandable. Most people would harshly punish someone in his shoes. But not him.

As an agent, he knew true criminals. But this kid? His tattered clothes and malnourished body told him everything he needed to know. He was doing this to survive.

And now that he was caught red-handed, what was the boy going to do? Would he continue feigning ignorance or cooperate? Or was he going to fight like a cornered rat? He hoped for the middle ground, but expected the other two scenarios, especially the last one.

As he patiently waited, he wasn't surprised by the fighting spirit. But how he used it... With surprising speed and precision, the boy kicked his latte out of his hand—straight into his face.

Having not expected it, his grip on the boy's wrist loosened, and he broke free. Quickly wiping his drink out of his eyes, he made chase. No way was he going to let him escape after that.

Weaving through traffic, Kirk followed him down multiple alleyways. A couple of times, he almost had him again, but then he'd sharply turn down another path. Again and again this would happen, and all he could feel towards the boy was admiration and frustration.

Was this kid trained by a thieving ninja or something!? Out of all the years he's pursued criminals, he'd never dealt with anything like this. Either they were too fast to catch and had to find another way, or he would have already taken them down. *Is he messing with me?*

Starting to think that was the case, Kirk followed him around another corner and came to an abrupt halt. He had disappeared. A quick look around revealed no clues as to where he went. Where did he go?

Not willing to give up, he carefully searched for any clues as to which direction he had gone. A footprint. A piece of torn clothing. Anything. But after checking everywhere, he found nothing. It was as though the boy vanished into thin air.

Is he even human? Deciding to put that thought on the back burner, he began heading down every path and asking anyone he came across if they had seen that dirty-blonde-haired, blue-eyed boy. To his dismay, none had. At least, none that were willing to speak to him.

Thanks to his job, he knew how to hunt down criminals of all types. Murderers. Thieves. Illegal tradesmen. A young pickpocket shouldn't be any different. All he needed was his usual hauntings and a clue as to where he tended to disappear to. Kirk let out a groan.

There goes my relaxing vacation.

***

"Alright. Thank you for your time."

Pushing back the disappointment of once again not getting another clue to the boy's—Sheen's, as he had gathered thus far—whereabouts, Kirk continued on. By what he'd found out, Sheen was an enigmatic child, even around the area he haunted. Those who knew him best claimed he had appeared out of the blue two years ago.

When he had, Sheen smelled of salty water, filthy, and a bit bloody—like he had gotten hurt and been tossed into the Mediterranean Sea. Some even remembered him pleading for help. As Kirk predicted, nobody did. The next thing they knew, he had turned to a life of crime.

Many believed that someone had taken him in and taught him how to steal. Though nobody knew for sure, it would make sense with how quickly he apparently learned to do it right. Others were certain he was scoping out marks with his pleading act. Kirk doubted the latter, but he couldn't rule it out until he found out for himself.

He was pondering everything he had learned thus far when a police officer—*polizia*, as they were called here—approached him. "I have been told you're looking for a little pickpocket, no?"

Kirk gave a nod. "I am. He looks to be about nine or ten, with dirty-blond hair and blue eyes. Fair-skinned. Have you seen him?"

"*Sì.* I have seen him."

Excitement sparked. "You have?"

"*Sì, signore.*"

"Where?"

"Around the area. Though we have recently been told of a group of *scugnizzo* living in an old cinema. I do believe that description matches one of them."

This could be the breakthrough I've been hoping for.

"That's wonderful news. Are you heading there now?"

The officer's eyes narrowed with understandable weariness. "I merely came to you to find out *why* you are looking for him."

"Not for anything bad, I can assure you. But two days ago, he stole my wallet. I'd like to get it back, if possible, and try to get him out of this life of crime before it destroys his life." Kline pulled out his badge—fortunately, he never kept it in his wallet—and showed it to the officer. "I'd hate to see another ruined when there was a chance to stop it."

"I see. Besides trying to find him, may I ask what you are doing in Rome, Agent Kline?"

"I was on vacation before the boy pulled his little stunt." Kirk could see the officer debating what to do. "I swear. I just want my wallet back—and to help him find a better way to live before this becomes his whole life."

Silence stretched on before the officer gave a stiff nod. "I shall allow it—only if you promise to listen and not act unless I tell you to."

"I promise Officer..."

"De Santis."

"Then, it's good to officially make your acquaintance, Officer De Santis." Kirk held out his hand.

Taking it in kind, Officer De Santis responded, "*Piacere mio,* Agent Kline."

With a mutual agreement, Kirk followed him. After some time, they reached a building that looked as though it had been purposely designed to sit half-sunken into the ground—an architectural wonder in its own right. The name emblazoned above the entrance read *Cinema Airone.* He let out a low whistle of impressed satisfaction.

"Have to say," Kirk commented, "even you guys' rundown buildings look like masterpieces." He glanced at his temporary partner. "So what's the plan on getting in without being spotted?"

"Come," Officer De Santis replied. "I will show you." Going to one of the sides, they found a missing window and peered in. Nobody—though they could hear yelling from what Kline figured was probably the main theater room.

Dropping inside, they carefully made their way towards the raised voices. The voice was deep, like an adult male. As they got closer, Kirk was surprised to hear that whoever it was wasn't speaking French but English. Was this man an American?

"You worthless urchin!" The voice roared as they neared the room. "I gave you a week to do what I asked, and this is all you've got!?"

Kline's lips thinned as he heard the sound of a small body hitting the ground after a resounding *smack*. He hated the thought of any child being treated this way—but it was a reality some had to face. Sadly, even to some who *do* have family.

"Leave him alone!" Kirk's eyes widened as he recognized that young voice. *Sheen*. Peering around the corner, there he was—standing between an enraged man and a cowering boy not much younger. Further away, more children huddled together, quivering in fear as the scene played out.

"Back off, Sheen!" the man sneered. "He needs to learn his lesson."

"No!" Sheen snapped back. "You're not touching him."

Kirk's jaw dropped in awe. Even though Sheen's trembling voice betrayed his fear, he still stood his ground. He had some backbone to him. One that he rarely saw in adults, let alone children.

"Touch!?" The man grabbed the front of Sheen's shirt, lifting him until their faces were nearly level. "I'm the reason you brats are alive—and clothed. I'm the reason you had food while I taught you how to steal to survive. And how do you repay me?"

"I-I stole enough to cover for him," Sheen quivered.

"And you think that makes up for his incompetence!?"

Kirk clenched his hands as he watched the man toss Sheen to the ground and plant his foot on the boy's chest. He knew what the man was doing. He'd seen this tactic before—used to break someone's spirit and force compliance.

If this was how they were always treated, no wonder he ran. And with no other adult giving him the time of day... Kirk hoped they weren't too late to do some good for the strong-willed boy.

The man leaned in, pressing harder. "All I asked was a measly eighty-five euros a week from each of you. That should be easy with the skills I taught all of you."

"He's still new," Sheen whispered.

"Five months is more than enough, and you know it," the man snapped. "You know what I think the problem is?" Glaring at the quivering child, he went on. "Laziness. And you, of all people, know how I hate laziness."

Fear clenched Kirk's heart as the man moved toward the cowering child. There was no mistaking his intent. He was going to beat the boy—and he had to be stopped before that happened.

He took a step forward to intervene, but Officer De Santis grabbed his arm, leaning in to whisper a sharp command. "No. Protect the children. If you attack him, I'll have to put cuffs on you too."

Forcing himself to rein in his emotions—as he always did in the field—he gave a reluctant nod and whispered back, his voice cold and controlled. "Then you'd best keep him away from me when I do. Or all bets are off."

Surprise flickered across the officer's face, but Kirk didn't care. No one had the right to treat children this way, no matter where they came from. It was one of the reasons he'd chosen to work for the FBI—when he wasn't assigning missions to his employees at Truth Corporation.

With a stiff nod, Officer De Santis turned his attention back to the scene. "Wait until we have an opening." Kirk agreed. If they rushed in too soon, the man could easily use the boy as a shield. They needed to catch him off guard—long enough to get the children out of the way.

They were still waiting when Sheen suddenly grabbed a small metal pipe and charged. The man's attention snapped to the approaching boy. He caught the pipe mid-swing, sneering. "You rebellious little fool!" On the last word, he backhanded him. The cowering child—the man's original target—scrambled away, retreating to the others.

Sheen hit the ground with an audible *oomph*, sliding nearly a foot across the pavement. The man tossed the "weapon" aside and stormed after him, roaring with fury as he began to beat him. Kirk shot a quick glance at the officer and felt a surge of relief when De Santis gave a sharp, decisive nod. Go time.

With no time to waste, Kirk swiftly and quietly rushed out. He had to make his approach carefully, or Sheen would be in immediate danger. Having been trained by a top scout back in the day, he had no trouble doing so. He only hoped that the cowering children and De Santis didn't give him away.

When he was nearly about to reach the boy, he heard the heavy footfalls of the officer approaching. And so did the man. Using that to his advantage, he slipped past, scooping up Sheen as he moved away.

"Fermati!" De Santis barked as Kirk bolted toward the other children. The man swore as the sound of a second set of heavy footsteps, running in the opposite direction, met his ears. He was trying to flee.

Come on, get 'em! He was halfway there when the crash of bodies colliding made him glance back. Officer De Santis had tackled the criminal to the ground. *Good.*

"You!?" Kirk's attention snapped to the wide-eyed boy in his arms. "What are you doing here?"

"Saving your rebellious hide," he scoffed before gentling his expression. "Can you move?"

Blinking his eyes a few times, Sheen regained his composure and shoved him away as he scrambled out of his arms. "I've had worse." As if his body disagreed, he let out a pained grunt as he clutched his right shoulder.

Alarm flared. Kirk stepped back in front of him, pushed his hand aside, and tugged his shirt just enough to reveal an old, angry scar on his right shoulder—faded at the edges, thick with healed tissue. A gunshot wound. Long past, but unmistakable.

Kirk's breath caught as he shifted the fabric slightly and spotted the smaller exit scar behind it. He was shot from behind. Not today. Not by this man. But still...

His gaze lifted to Sheen's face, questions bombarding his thoughts. Whatever this kid's story was, it was darker—and far older—than this.

He didn't have time to ask as Sheen smacked his hands away, scrambling back. Raw fear warring with fury across his face. The reaction was immediate, instinctive—too sharp for a simple boundary crossed. Kirk froze, understanding settling in like a weight. He'd crossed a line that he didn't know existed.

"It's okay. It's okay." Kirk raised his hands in surrender, backing off a step as he tried to calm him. "I'm sorry. I was just worried he might've done something to hurt you that badly."

"He didn't!" Sheen snapped. "So back off!"

"I'm trying to help."

"Help?" Sheen scoffed. "Nobody cares about kids like us. That's why we ended up with him."

"You ended up with him because none of you ever met someone who would've helped." The look on the boy's face made it clear he didn't believe a word of it.

This is getting me nowhere. Kirk was about to try a different approach when something caught his eye. Glancing down, he spotted a pure white feather lying in the grime—nearly the size of an eagle's. Strangely, it wasn't bent, trampled, or stained the way it should've been. Did it belong to the kid?

Curious, he slowly picked it up. The moment his fingers closed around it, a powerful sensation washed over him, stealing his breath. The feeling wasn't malicious or threatening—it was calm. Peaceful. Comforting. One of which he hadn't felt in a long time.

It felt like... like coming home. Loved, the way his mother, half-sister, and aunt used to hold him. Protected, the way his stepfather and uncle always stood at his side. Wanted, the way his wife had looked at him, as if losing him was unthinkable. Feelings from a life that no longer existed.

A moment passed as he realized something wet rolling down his cheeks. Tears. He'd thought he'd cried his last the day they died. Apparently, he'd been wrong.

When he looked up, Sheen was staring at him in open disbelief. Why? Was he the only other one who could feel this? Were they more alike than either of them realized?

***

Is he... just like me?

Sheen took a deep breath and stared at the stranger. For the past two years, anyone who touched his feather had recoiled from it—always complaining that it felt scary or wrong. Bad. But this man... he hadn't done any of that.

Hesitantly, he took a step closer. Fear rooted his feet to the floor a heartbeat later. What if the crying man yelled at him? What if he blamed him for whatever was happening?

Sheen swallowed and forced another shaky breath through his nose. Then he moved again. In only a few steps, he stood in front of him. The man's eyes were still wet when they met Sheen's, and what he saw there made his chest ache. Grief. Deep and heavy. The kind that never really went away. He had lost everyone he cared about.

Something in Sheen's chest pulled toward him—toward the pain they somehow shared. But was that enough to trust him? His head said no. It always said no. Still... something inside him hesitated.

"I-Is this yours?" The man asked.

Sheen gave a slow nod. "I found it next to me after I woke up. Two years ago."

The man smiled—not big, not forced. Just sad and gentle. "Then you found a very special feather." He held it out to him. "Try not to lose it. Okay?"

With that, the last of Sheen's questioning dissipated. He *could* be trusted. Taking the feather, he flung his arms around the surprised man. "They're still in your heart." After a moment longer, his hug was returned.

***

Should I? Leaning against the wall of the cinema, Kirk contemplated what to do about Sheen. The boy wasn't just brave—he was also wise for his age. A combination that was hard to find.

They're still in your heart.

A wisp of a smile crossed his face as he remembered the boy's words. He hadn't told the boy anything of his past, but he had known anyway. Like he'd lived through something similar himself. Was that where he'd got that wound?

His thoughts were interrupted by a few choice words flying out of the criminal's mouth as the man was forced into the back of a police car. After everything he had seen, Kirk was glad the man was going to be behind bars. No kid deserved to be treated that way. Not in his book.

Relieved when the door slammed shut, he shifted his attention to the orphanage lady, who was speaking gently to the children they'd rescued. The kids were weary, but she was patient, willing to move at their pace. All except one. The one who had disappeared when Officer De Santis's team arrived. Sheen.

Up until then, the caring, protective boy had been calming the other kids—giving them hope and helping Kirk approach without any of them cowering away. He had even begun to think he'd earned the boy's full trust. But now... was there no getting through to him at all?

When the rest of De Santis' team arrived, Sheen had slipped away. Kirk had hoped he had just gone to get a few things. But that had been fifteen minutes ago. The place was big—but not *that* big. Did he really not want a different life?

He was starting to think the answer was no when movement off to his left caught his attention. To his pleasant surprise, it was Sheen. The boy stopped a few steps away, looking nervous. What could he still be nervous about?

Before Kirk could ask, Sheen shyly spoke. "Here. I'm sorry for taking it." He held out the wallet.

Warmed by the gesture, Kirk smiled as he took it. "All's forgiven." He ruffled the kid's hair. "Thanks for returning it."

Sheen giggled and smiled up at him. It amazed him how a child who had endured so much could still smile so brightly. He was truly a special kid. One that he believed would benefit from the program he and his partner had been approved for.

But would he want it if offered the chance? It was hard to tell. Kirk knew the boy would be a natural. What concerned him more was whether Sheen would be willing to separate from the other kids.

Sheen's smile faltered as his attention drifted elsewhere. Following his gaze, he realized he was watching the orphanage lady. The other children had moved closer to her now, visibly more relaxed. That was a good sign. So what was troubling him?

The answer came with Sheen's next words. "I wish I didn't have to go with her. But I guess I have no choice, huh." Hearing exactly the opening he needed, Kirk suppressed the excitement bubbling up within.

"If you don't want to go with the others, then you don't have to," he said with a small shrug. "I'm not gonna force you."

"What choice do I have? I don't want to steal anymore."

"I'm glad to hear that," Kirk said gently. "But there *is* another option. One I can help with—if you're interested."

"I don't know." Sheen studied him wearily. "I guess it depends on what it is."

"Fair answer." Kirk straightened. "And I think it's time I introduced myself. I'm Kirk Kline. A Special Agent for the United States of America."

Sheen's jaw dropped. "You're from America?"

"That's correct. And just recently, my partner and I started a program for kids who've been through things like you— teaching them skills they can use to help others. Some might even choose to become agents one day, if they want to learn."

Sheen cocked his head in confusion. "What do agents do?"

"Our job is to protect the innocent from those who wish to do others harm—and to stop illegal sales."

"Illegal? Like what?"

"Things that are dangerous—or just not okay to sell. We've even stopped bad people from selling other people." His voice hardened slightly. "That's never okay. Not in America."

Sheen's expression became one of awe. "So agents are like superheroes?"

Kirk chuckled, relaxing his stance. "I guess we would be considered a type of hero."

"And you want to teach *me* to be one too?"

"That's correct. But I will be honest with you, Sheen." Kirk knelt down to meet his eyes. "Being this kind of hero is a thankless job. It can be hard at times."

"But why?"

"Because we can't risk being known by too many bad people. If we are, we can't keep helping others."

"Is that why you're called a *Special* Agent? Because you have to be invisible to everyone?"

"I'm afraid so."

Sheen's smile returned in full bloom, pride puffing up his chest. "Then I'm special to get the chance to see you." His enthusiasm dimmed slightly. "But... are you sure you want to teach me?"

Kirk smiled. "You *are* special, Sheen. And that feather of yours—it matters. That's why I'm offering. Do you want to learn how to become an agent?"

His excitement surged back instantly. He nodded hard. "Yes! I want to be an invisible hero like you and save *lots* of people. I can't wait to go back to America and learn how to be like you!"

Kline's eyes widened. "Back!? You mean... you're from America?" He knew the boy looked American, but he thought that his parents had probably moved here before he was born.

"Uh-huh." He watched as Sheen's excitement faded as he continued to talk about his past. "But then my parents made me go with them. And we were traveling with a big group of people on the other side of the big water. I think they called it a caravan?"

"Big water? Caravan?" Realization struck Kirk. "Are you talking about the Mediterranean Sea?"

"Uh-huh. That's what my parents called it. Until Bad men with guns attacked us."

So that's when he got shot.

Kirk's heart sank as the pieces fell into place. "How did you escape?"

"I fell into the water when my shoulder got hurt." Sheen started to sniffle as tears began to stream down his face. "I don't remember what happened after that. I woke up on an island close to here... and found the feather."

Unable to hold back any longer, Kirk wrapped his arms around the boy, letting him cry it out. Something he doubted Sheen had much time to do since he got here. He let out a heavy breath.

"You carry a heavy burden for one so young," he murmured.

***

A few days had passed since the incident, and Kirk was back on U.S. soil with his first member of the program. After Sheen had calmed down, he showed him some of the things that he managed to escape with. One of them was his U.S. passport. Convenient for them.

He even learned that the boy's last name was Wilder. A perfect name for him—at least in Kirk's opinion—after finding out how he gave him the slip. He had apparently climbed up and hidden on top of a ledge until he ran down another passage—then headed back the way they'd entered from. Classic.

Grabbing their bags from the baggage claim, Kirk grinned at his young friend. "Ready?"

"Uh-huh," Sheen answered as he watched people hustle by. "They do realize they're easy pickings for a thief, right?"

Kirk chuckled as he shook his head. "Best keep those little hands from teaching them, unless you want to be thrown in jail. Or get me in trouble. Let's go."

They left the baggage claim and headed into the multi-level parking garage. Getting into the elevator, they went up a couple of floors and stepped out. As he did, he spotted his car right where he left it. But now, a familiar man was leaning against it. He was staring right at them with the biggest grin Kirk had seen in a while.

"Who's he?" Sheen whispered.

Grinning, Kirk replied, "Harold Sanders. My partner." Seeing the surprise in the boy's eyes, he knew it was high time to introduce them.

Making his way over, Kirk teased, "And here I thought you'd be waiting till our vacation's officially over to want anything to do with me."

"And miss my favorite partner's arrival with our first little recruit?" Harold chuckled as he pushed off the car. "Not a chance."

"Figures I'd be because of the kid."

"Ah, get over here." Laughing aloud, they gave each other a welcoming hug. "It's good to see you again, my friend."

"Likewise." They let go, still smiling like two old goofballs. "How was Jason's birthday?"

"Great. You should've seen his eyes light up when he unwrapped his first hammer. He wanted to try it out right then and there."

"Stopped him before he tried to 'fix' something that didn't need it?"

"And before Martha used it to 'fix' my head." They burst out laughing. Martha Sanders was a tough and caring woman. In truth, Kirk had always thought that Harold was a lucky guy to have a woman like that.

Harold turned his attention to Kirk's side. "And you must be Sheen Wilder." Kirk turned to see Sheen wearily watching them. He became alarmed when his partner held out his hand. "It's good to finally meet you."

Seeing the fight or flight reaction tensing the boy's body, Kirk quickly stepped in. "Sheen? Would you like to see how my partner reacts to holding your special feather?"

Harold gave Kirk a confused look before kneeling in front of Sheen and playing along. "A *special* feather? Sounds cool. Can I see it?"

Sheen cautiously glanced between them before slowly pulling out his feather. Kirk moved beside the boy as he handed it over to

Harold. Immediately, he gasped as he stared at it. A moment later, his attention snapped to Kirk.

"It caught me off guard too," Kirk scoffed.

With a slow nod, Harold turned his attention back to Sheen. "This really *is* special."

"How do you feel?" Sheen quietly asked, seemingly wanting to know.

"Honestly, I'm not fully sure. I feel like... I want to keep it close, like a lifeline. But I also feel like dropping it because of how overwhelming it is."

"Do you think it's bad?"

"No." Harold shook his head. "Just overwhelming. Like I'm safe and being given a loving peace. Is this how you feel with it?"

"I always want to hold it close. Because without it... I-I'm so scared."

Harold gave an understanding smile as he handed it back. "Then hold on tight to it, Sheen."

He had pulled it close and let out a sigh of relief. Then, to the boy's surprise, Harold wrapped Sheen in a hug. "You're not alone anymore. And you're not going to be treated like you were in Rome— if I have anything to say about it. I promise."

Kirk smiled. He knew his partner meant it. He loved children and would do anything to protect them. He didn't know if it was because of his own son or what. But whatever the reason, it made him the wonderful man he was.

He was glad to see that Sheen could see it too.

The End

About the Author

Tina Linn has always loved stories that blend adventure with heart, exploring courage, compassion, and the choices that shape our lives. With a passion for crafting worlds where characters grow and discover their strength, Tina invites readers to journey alongside heroes both ordinary and extraordinary.

When she's not writing, Tina enjoys camping, hiking, fishing, reading, and so much more while discovering the little wonders hidden in everyday life; sharing stories with friends and family.

Other Works by Tina Linn

- *The First Hike* (Short Story)

- *The Veiled Path* (Short Story)

- *The Enigmatic Pickpocket* (Short Story)

- *Coming soon in July*: The World Unknown, Book One: Drawn Beyond the Veil

- *Coming soon in October*: The World Unknown, Book Two: Scorpions at the Edge of Sleep

- *Coming soon January of next year*: The World Unknown, Book Three: Fractured Worlds

Thank you for reading *The Space Between Choices Collection*. Your support means the world, and we hope these stories inspire you to reflect, grow, and embrace the choices that shape your journey.

www.ingramcontent.com/pod-product-compliance
Lightning Source LLC
Chambersburg PA
CBHW051458140726
47987CB00006B/2761